The Little book of Adoption

a candid look at life through the eyes of adoptees

Heather Waters

Author Heather Waters

Illustrations Ellie Turner

Table of Contents

Baby Oni

The first moments of separation cause panic and anxiety. The effects of the event remain for all Oni's life. The result of the trauma causes Oni to constantly be in a state of vigilance – alert, which in turn has a detrimental effect on all future relationships and Oni's health.

Mirroring

I look in the mirror,

Who do I see?

Do I see me?

?

I don't know

Who I look like.

A vision of you?

A vision of who?

Who is it

That I'm supposed

To see?

Is that me?

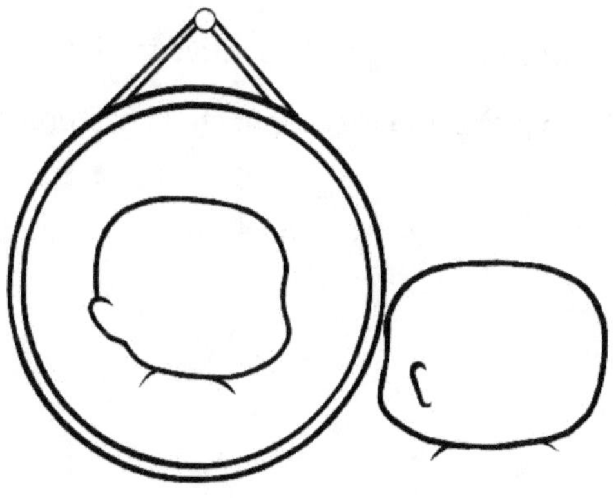

Family/Ancestry

I don't fit here

Trying to find a connection with family and adoptive family trees; with biological family ~ to find a place and feel connected both present and past …

The search for identity

fog

I'm so grateful

I was chosen

I'm fine

I have a family

I'm not going to search

I don't need to know anything about myself

I'll wait until my adoptive parents have died

This (you) needs to be kept secret

siblings

are you my sister

are you my brother

not feeling like I fit here

you are my sister

you are my brother

i don't connect with you

i do not fit here

Medical

Doctor: Does any of your family have this condition?

Oni: ......

Birth Certificate

Here is your "amended" Birth Certificate

You can get your Original Birth Certificate when you're an adult
~ depending on where you live

You cannot use your Original Birth Certificate for identification.
It is not a legal document. It has been

CANCELLED

Belonging

Always searching for a place to belong in most things

birthdays

Christmas, Mother's Day or special occasions

Expected to be excited

But feeling glum

Days of loss

Intercountry

Assumptions that Oni looks foreign so Oni was born foreign

foreign language

Oni looks foreign so Oni must understand the language and culture

Schoolyard

We can always **send you back!**

You're a **BASTARD**

BLOOD is thicker than water

That's so cool. **I wish I was adopted**

Your parents **CHOSE** you

Your mother **didn't want you**

I **didn't want** to adopt, it was your father's idea

You're **lucky**. You should be **grateful**

Don't you want to meet your **REAL** mum?

You **don't belong there**. You can run away

They're not your **REAL** parents

Psychologist

P: "what brings you here today"

Oni: "First, I'll let you know that I'm adopted"

P: "I had an adopted client once"

Counsellors

"let's focus

on the here

and now"

Legalities

Adoptive Parents: We want a different one

Welfare: Sure, we will take this one from you

Oni: I want to discharge my adoption

Welfare: You need apply to the court, it will cost you $$$, you need to prove good reason for discharge, require permission from your adopters, you'll need to find 3 people to verify ....

You're not part of this family. There is nothing in the Will for you

We cannot issue you a **passport** if you don't have your biological father's birth certificate

Oni: I want to open a bank account

Teller: We can't use this *birth certificate* as **identification, it's been cancelled**

Reunion

Maybe I finally belong
What if I don't like her
What if I don't fit in
You're a stranger to me
I can't wait to meet my siblings
What if she doesn't like me
What if they don't like me
Where is my dad?
Will I meet my dad?
I knew I'd find you some day
What if ...
What if he doesn't like me

Oni

These things happened to me

I give myself permission to feel

These feelings are a normal reaction to an abnormal situation

My situation has given me coping skills

I matter

I belong

I am okay

I am worthy

I am normal

I am real

I am...

ONI

Creators

Heather Waters

Author

Ellie Turner

Illustrator

About the Author

Heather Waters, mother of two daughters, grand-mother to five, has been an advocate for adoptees over the past twenty years. She has studied trauma and colour therapies, researched issues on abandonment, anxiety, rejection, shame, trust and more. She commenced professional film producing in 2012 with multi award winning short, The Lost Souls. She has since won multiple awards on documentaries; You Should be Grateful and You Were Chosen.

Bye